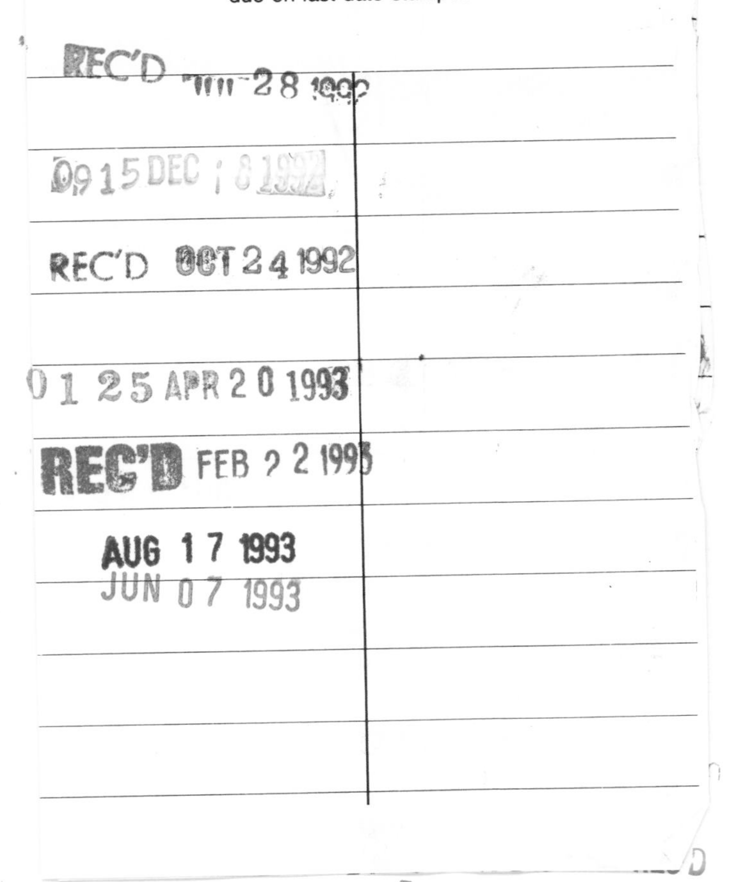

REC'D
DEC 8 1992
REC'D OCT 24 1992
APR 20 1993
REC'D FEB 22 1993
AUG 17 1993
JUN 07 1993

THE ADVENTURES OF LITTLE MOUK

BY WILHELM HAUFF
TRANSLATED AND ADAPTED BY ELIZABETH SHUB
ILLUSTRATED BY MONIKA LAIMGRUBER

MACMILLAN PUBLISHING CO., INC.
NEW YORK

Macmillan Publishing Co., Inc.
866 Third Avenue, New York, N.Y. 10022
Printed in Switzerland
1 2 3 4 5 6 7 8 9 10

Library of Congress Cataloging in Publication Data
Shub, Elizabeth. The adventures of little Mouk.
An adaptation of W. Hauff's Der kleine Muck. [1. Fairy tales]
I. Hauff, Wilhelm, 1802-1827. Der kleine Muck.
II. Laimgruber, Monika, illus. III. Title.
PZ8.S34515Ad3 [E] 74-4420 ISBN 0-02-743400-1

Moukrah, or "Little Mouk" as he was called, lived with his father in a small town in Turkey. It happened that Mouk had stopped growing at an early age, and when the time came, his father decided not to send him to school. Father and son lived a hermit-like existence and the boy remained child-like and ignorant of the world. When Mouk was sixteen, his father had a bad fall and died of his injuries. Some relatives to whom he was in debt took over his house. They told Mouk, who was left penniless, that he must go out into the world and seek his fortune.

Mouk cheerfully agreed, asking only for some of his father's clothes to wear on the journey. These he received, but his father had been a tall, stout man and the clothes were too big. Mouk quickly cut the trouser legs to shorten them. They were still too wide, so he tied his father's broad sash around his waist. That held them up, and he thought no more about it. He put on his father's blue jacket and turban, and stuck his father's long Damascus dagger jauntily into his sash. He picked up a stick and set out, a bizarre figure indeed.

He walked contentedly the first day, knowing he was on his way to seek his fortune. Whatever he saw pleased him, even a piece of broken glass sparkling in the sunlight. Perhaps it would turn into a diamond, he thought, and quickly picked it up. Fire-like rays reflected from the dome of a distant mosque, a lake blinking like a far-away mirror made him hurry joyfully forward to what he believed was a magical city. But as he ran, the fiery dome and mirror lake faded away as if they had never been. He saw his mistake, and his tired feet and empty grumbling stomach brought him back to the reality of a stony road and gnawing hunger.

In this way he travelled for two days, eating only whatever berries and greens he could gather in the fields, and at night sleeping on the hard ground. He began to wonder if he would ever find his fortune.

On the evening of the third day, he wearily followed the road uphill. But when he reached the top he saw, in the valley below, a large city, its domes and minarets gleaming in the moonlight.

"If I don't find my luck there, I won't find it anywhere," Mouk said to himself; and, hopeful once again, he trudged on. The city had seemed quite close, but it was some time before Mouk finally arrived at its gate. He walked through the strange streets. There was no one to greet him, no one to offer him food or a place to rest.

Just as he stopped to look longingly at a large rich house, a casement flew open and an old lady called out in a singsong voice:

"Come, everyone,
The dinner's done,
There's a clean white cloth,
And bread and broth,
The stew's a treat,
Come all and eat."

The door of the house was opened wide and soon a crowd of cats and dogs came running towards it. Mouk hesitated for a moment, wondering what he should do. Finally he screwed up his courage and decided to follow two young cats who he thought would surely know the way to the kitchen. As he walked up to the door, the old woman appeared. She gave him a surly look and asked grumpily what he was doing there.

"You said, 'Come all and eat,'" Mouk replied. "And I'm so hungry."

The old woman laughed and said, "You're an odd sight, you are. You must be a stranger. The whole town knows that I cook only for my dear cats and once in a while I ask their friends to join us."

Mouk told the old lady about what had happened to him and asked if she would let him eat with her cats just this once. The old lady liked his frankness and gave him as much food as he could eat. And when he had finished, she said: "Why don't you stay here and work for me? You won't have much to do. The lodging is comfortable and the food is good and I will pay you a small wage in addition."

Mouk, with the taste of the delicious stew still in his mouth, agreed to stay. The job the old lady gave him was easy enough. Mrs. Ahavzi, as she was called, had two toms and four female cats. It was Mouk's job to brush the cats each morning

and rub a special salve into their coats. He had to watch them when the old lady went out, serve their bowls of food at mealtime, and at night put them to bed on their velvet cushions and tuck them under their silken coverlets. There were also several small dogs in the house to be taken care of, but no such great fuss was made over them. For the rest, Mouk led just as lonely a life as he had in his father's house.

With the exception of Mrs. Ahavzi, he saw only the cats and dogs the day long.

For a while all went well. Mouk had plenty to eat, light work to do, and Mrs. Ahavzi was very pleased with him. But as time went on, the cats began to get restless. As soon as the old lady would leave the house, they ran around the rooms as if possessed, upsetting the furniture and breaking any dish that stood in their way.

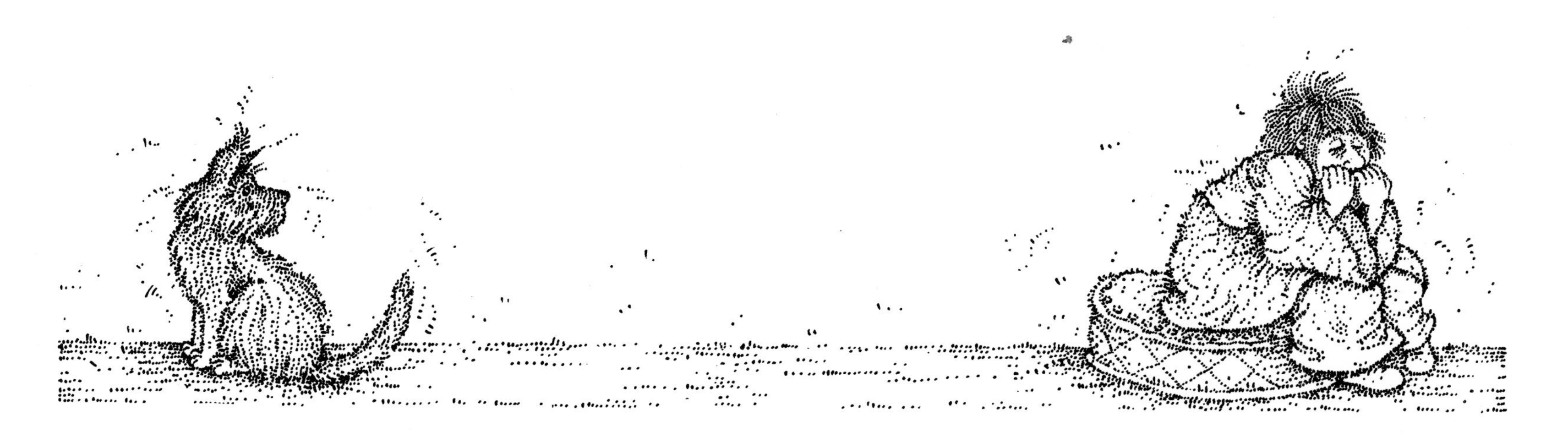

No sooner did they hear their mistress's footsteps coming up the stairs than they ran to their cushions and sat there, waving their tails in greeting, as if nothing at all had taken place in her absence. Mrs. Ahavzi flew into a rage when she saw the disorder her rooms were in and blamed Mouk for everything, though, of course, it was all the cats' doing.

Mouk saw that he had no future there and decided it was time to leave. He had no money and by now he had learned how difficult it was to get along without it. Mrs. Ahavzi had promised to pay him, but she had not kept her word. Mouk tried to think of a way to get the money she owed him, since he knew that asking for it would do no good. There was a room in the house that was always kept locked, and Mouk guessed it must be where the old lady kept her valuables. But how could he get into that room?

One morning when the old lady went out, one of the small dogs whom Mouk especially liked to play with tugged at his broad trousers. The dog seemed to be inviting him to follow, and Mouk did. The dog led him into the old lady's bedroom and stopped in front of a small door which Mouk had never noticed before, and which now stood partly open. The dog ran through the door and Mouk went after him. He was happily surprised to find himself in Mrs. Ahavzi's secret room.

He looked around to see if he could find any money, but there was none. There were various objects, a chest, old clothes, and odd jugs and dishes. A crystal bowl with figures etched into it caught Mouk's eye and he picked it up. As he did so, its cover fell off and shattered into bits. For a moment he stood there petrified. He knew what a beating was in store for him when the old lady discovered what had happened, and wisely decided to leave before she returned. He looked around one last time to see if there wasn't something that would be useful on his journey.

A pair of shoes caught his eye. They had upward-pointing toes and they were

enormous. Still, they were better than his own shoes, the soles of which were worn to holes. He quickly took his old shoes off and pushed his feet into the giant ones. A battered walking stick, with a carved lion's head for a handle, leaned against the chest, and Mouk took it along as he left the room. Quickly he went to his own room, put on his blue coat and his turban, stuck the Damascus dagger into his sash, and ran out of the house, through the streets to the city gates.

Once out of the city, he continued to run until he thought he couldn't take another step. He had never run so fast in his life and it seemed to him that some hidden force was carrying him forward. At last he realized that he was not running at all but that his shoes were running him. He tried in every way to stop them, but the giant shoes skimmed swiftly along. Finally, not knowing what to do, he cried out, "Whoa! Whoa!" as if to a horse. The shoes stopped at once. Mouk dropped exhausted to the ground and in a moment was fast asleep.

He dreamed that the little dog who had led him to Mrs. Ahavzi's secret room came to him and said, "You're not using your shoes properly. If you want them to

work for you, this is what you must do: When you put them on, make sure to turn three times on your heel, then say where you want to go and the shoes will fly you there. And that walking stick you have is not just for walking. It can find hidden treasures. When it taps three times, that's where gold is buried; twice means silver."

When Mouk awoke, he remembered his dream and decided to test it. He put on the giant shoes, placed his weight on one heel, and tried to turn around. But in those shoes it was easier said than done. He fell on his face more than once, but he kept on trying until at last he managed to make the turns. He immediately wished himself in the nearest large city. The shoes carried him into the air, through the clouds, and soon landed him in a crowded marketplace with people busily rushing about and many booths displaying their wares. He was pushed and shoved. His shoes got stepped on, his long dagger got in the way, and Mouk had to force his way out of the market in search of a safer place.

He found a quiet street and walked along thinking about the best way to earn some money. He thought first of his stick, but the city was large and he didn't know where to look. It might take a long time to locate a treasure. It occurred to him that the best way to make use of his flying shoes would be as a messenger. He decided to go to the palace and offer his services there. He asked a passerby the way and when he came to the palace gate, inquired for the steward in charge of the king's servants.

When the steward heard what Mouk wanted, he looked him up and down and said: "With legs as short as yours, you'd be about as fast as a snail. I'm not here to joke with every fool that comes along. You're wasting my time. Get out of my sight before I throw you out!"

Mouk, however, insisted that he was prepared to prove himself by running a race with the fastest royal messenger. The idea struck the steward as very funny. Such a race, he thought, would surely provide an unusual entertainment for the king. He told Mouk to be prepared to race that very evening and took him to the kitchens where he was given food and drink. He himself went to tell the king about the race.

The king liked a good joke and was delighted with the prospect of witnessing such a ridiculous event. He ordered the steward to set up a course in a huge meadow behind the palace.

Word of the race spread quickly, and by sunset everyone flocked to the meadow, where stands had been erected so that all could see the contest between the boasting dwarf and the king's best runner.

When the royal family and their entourage had settled themselves in the reviewing stand, Mouk came out and bowed formally to the entire company. Cheers and peals of laughter greeted his appearance. It was difficult not to laugh at the small figure in its outlandish clothes. But Mouk paid no attention to the laughter. He stood there proudly, his stick in his hand, waiting for his opponent to get into position. The royal runner came out and placed himself at Mouk's side. Both waited for the starting signal from Princess Amarza. She waved her scarf, and like two arrows shot from the same bow the racers flew down the meadow.

At first the royal runner gained a considerable lead, but Mouk in his flying shoes soon caught up, overtook him, and had long since finished the course when his opponent, gasping for breath, arrived at the finish line. For a moment the spectators stared in disbelief. The king himself was the first to applaud, the crowd joined in, and all cheered: "Long live Little Mouk, the winner!"

Mouk was escorted to the king. He bowed low before him and said: "Your Highness, what I have shown you is only a small example of what I can do. All I ask is that you make me one of your royal messengers."

The king replied: "From now on you are not only one of the royal messengers, but I appoint you my own personal messenger and I will keep you always at my side. You will receive a hundred gold pieces a year as your wage, and you will sit at table with my chief stewards."

Mouk believed he had at last found his place in the world and was content. The king favoured Mouk and confided in him. He had never had so trusty and speedy a messenger.

However, it was not long before the king's attendants and stewards grew jealous of Mouk. They did not like playing second fiddle to one they considered an ignorant dwarf, whose only accomplishment was to run fast. They constantly plotted to make Mouk fall out of favour with the king, but they could not shake the king's confidence in his tiny messenger.

Mouk, who was very kind-hearted, did not try to revenge himself. Instead he wondered what he might do to win their approval. He hadn't thought much about his walking stick because he had everything he needed. But now it occurred to him that if the stick could help him find a treasure, he could share it with his enemies and they would surely be better disposed towards him. It was said that the king's father had had a treasure buried somewhere on the palace grounds when an invading army had overrun the country, and he had died before he could tell his son where the treasure was hidden.

Mouk began carrying his stick with him whenever he went out on the palace grounds, hoping that one day he would come across the hidden gold. And indeed, one evening as he walked in a remote part of the palace garden, he felt the stick moving in his hand as it tapped three times on the ground. He noted the spot, went back to the palace to get a spade, and waited for nightfall.

It was hard digging when he returned to the garden, but after two hours his spade hit something that clanged like metal. Excited, he dug faster and soon unearthed an iron lid. It covered a large urn filled with gold coins. Mouk tried to lift out the urn, but found he was not strong enough. Instead he filled his trouser pockets, took off his coat and carefully tied as many coins into it as it would hold. He replaced the lid of the urn, filled in the hole, and made his way back to the palace. The gold was so heavy it weighed him down. Had he not been wearing his magic shoes he would not have been able to get to his room.

Mouk in his innocence believed that now he could give such splendid gifts to his enemies that they would surely become his friends. But, of course, the more he gave them, the more he aroused their envy and suspicion.

Ahuli, the cook, accused him of being a counterfeiter.

Ahmet, the chief steward, announced that Mouk had surely flattered the king into giving him the money.

Archaz, the treasurer, who had himself been dipping into the king's money boxes, was quick to say that Mouk had stolen it.

They hatched a plan to see if they could find out how Mouk actually got the money.

One day the chief cupbearer appeared before the king. He looked so crestfallen that the king could not help noticing it and asked what troubled him.

"Alas," said the cupbearer. "I am sad because clearly I have lost the favour of the king."

"Nonsense, friend Korchuz," the king replied. "What makes you say that?"

"Because," said Korchuz, "you have rewarded your personal messenger with gold, but to your other servants and to me, your equally loyal cupbearer, you have given nothing."

The king was most astonished to hear this. Korchuz then related how Mouk was handing out money to everyone and it was easy enough to plant in the king's mind the thought that the likeliest source of the gold was the royal money coffers. The king at once ordered that Mouk be secretly followed wherever he went. If he was stealing from the treasury, he would soon be caught.

Meanwhile Mouk had given away all of his gold coins, and on the following night made his way to the remote garden where the money was buried in order to replenish his supplies. He did not know that he was being followed by the king's guards led by Ahuli, the cook, and Archaz, the treasurer. As soon as he had transferred the gold coins to his pockets and coat, he was grabbed, bound, and brought to the king. The king, who was annoyed because he had been awakened from his sleep, decided to try Mouk right then and there. The urn was immediately dug up,

and together with Mouk's spade and coat filled with gold coins, was placed in evidence before the king. Archaz stated that he and Ahuli and the guards had surprised Mouk as he was burying the urn filled with coins.

The king then asked the prisoner if this was so, and where he had found the gold.

Mouk simply told the truth—that he had discovered the treasure in the garden and was digging it up, and not trying to bury it.

All present laughed at Mouk's unlikely explanation, but the king, enraged by what he thought was rudeness, cried out: "Do you consider your king so stupid that you not only steal his money but make sport of him as well? Archaz, I demand to know at once whether a sum corresponding to this is missing from my treasury."

The treasurer, glad of the opportunity to cover himself, replied that an even greater sum was gone from the treasury and he swore that the coins in the urn were part of the missing money.

The king ordered that Mouk be put in chains and imprisoned in the palace tower. He gave the urn to Archaz and told him to put the money back where it belonged. Delighted that everything was going his way, the treasurer took the urn home to count the coins. At the bottom of the urn he found a note from the king's father which said:

> "The enemy has invaded my land, and therefore I have buried here a part of my fortune; whoever finds it will suffer the curse of his king if he does not immediately give it to my son.
> *King Sadi."*

Of course, Archaz told no one about the note and its contents.

Mouk sat miserably in his prison. He knew that the penalty for stealing from the king was death. Yet if he revealed the secrets of his walking stick and flying shoes, they would surely be taken from him. On the other hand, in his present situation neither was of any use to him. There was nothing in the prison for the stick to find and his short chains made it impossible to turn on his heel and wish himself away. And so, on the following day, when he received his sentence, he decided that it was better to part with stick and shoes and live than to keep them and die. He asked for a last audience with the king. It was granted, and Mouk said he would reveal his secret if the king would grant him his life in return. The king agreed. Mouk told him about the magic stick, and the king at once ordered that some gold be buried on the palace grounds and told Mouk to go out and find it. It was not long before the stick tapped three times on the right spot.

The king saw that his royal treasurer had lied to him. As was the custom at the time, he sent Archaz a silken rope, which meant he was to hang himself. Such an order from the king could not be disobeyed.

To Mouk the king said: "I have promised you your life, but it would seem to me that the secret of the stick is not the only one you possess. If you don't tell me as well what makes you able to run so swiftly, I will have you imprisoned for life." One night in the tower had been enough for Mouk and he had no desire to spend the rest of his life there. And so he told the king about the hidden power behind his shoes. However, he kept to himself the part about turning three times on his heel and the way to stop them running.

The king immediately asked to try the shoes. As soon as he put them on, they carried him crazily around the palace garden. They would not stop, and Mouk, who could not resist this small revenge, let the king run until he fell fainting to the ground.

When he revived, the king was furious. "I granted you your life and freedom," he said, "but if you are not out of the country in twelve hours I'll have you hanged."

Then he took Mouk's stick and shoes and sent them to be locked up in the royal treasury.

Again as poor as when he had left home, Mouk started out. The country he was leaving was not very large. Although he had become used to his magic shoes and found walking without them tiring, he arrived at the border in about eight hours. When he crossed over, he left the main road to look for a secluded spot in a forest where he could live alone and try to forget his disappointments. In a dense wood he came upon a clear stream shaded by trees, and a moss bank that seemed to invite him to stay. He threw himself down on the moss and despite his sad thoughts soon fell asleep.

When he awoke, he was very hungry. He looked about to see if he could find something to eat and discovered that tempting, ripe figs hung from the tree under which he had slept. He picked and ate some. Then he went to the stream to quench his thirst. He could not believe what he saw reflected in the water. Two mighty ears hung down at the sides of his head and his nose had grown thick and long. Panic-stricken, he put his hands to his head. The monstrous ears were really there.

"I've earned these donkey's ears," he cried out, "for like a donkey I have trampled my luck underfoot."

He wandered about beneath the trees, not knowing what to do. After a time he was hungry again and picked some more figs, this time from another tree.

When he had finished, it struck him that if he could force his ears underneath his turban he might look less ridiculous. He put his hands up to do so, only to feel that the huge ears were no longer there. He rushed to the stream, pulled off his turban, and found that his ears had gone back to normal. His nose too had returned to its former shape.

Now he understood what had taken place: The figs from the first tree had made his nose and ears grow, the figs from the second tree had cured him. Surely, he thought, these magic figs would somehow help him find his luck again. He picked as many figs from each of the trees as he could carry and turned back to the land which he had left only a short time ago. On his way he worked out a plan.

In the first village he came to, he exchanged his clothes for those of a beggar so that he would not be recognized, and continued on to the king's city.

It was a time of year when ripe fruit was scarce. Mouk took his stand outside the palace gate, among the peddlers from whom the kitchen steward bought foods for the king's table. He didn't have long to wait before the steward came out and looked around at what the peddlers had to sell. His eye fell on Mouk's basket of fresh ripe figs.

"Ah," he said. "The king will certainly be pleased to have these. What do you want for the whole basket?"

Mouk mentioned a reasonable price and the bargain was struck. Mouk left at once for the other end of the city. He did not want to be around when the ears and noses of the king and his household began to grow.

The king was in a very good mood at dinner and praised the steward for the delicacies he always managed to provide. And the steward was very pleased with himself because he knew what treat he still had in store and that the king would reward him for it. He smiled mysteriously and dropped such remarks as "The day has not yet had its evening," or "All's well that ends well," so that the princesses became especially curious about what delicious morsel was still to appear. When he finally placed the inviting basket of ripe figs on the table, a chorus of "ahs" could be heard from the company. The king, who was very frugal when it came to such rarities, portioned out the figs himself. Each prince and princess received two figs apiece and the ladies and viziers, one. The remainder he took for himself, and set about swallowing them with great relish.

Suddenly the Princess Amarza cried out, "Dear father, how strange you look!"

Everyone stared at the king in astonishment. Flapping ears hung from his head, a long nose drooped down to his chin. Then they looked at one another in shock and fear. The entire company had sprouted huge ears and long noses.

The court doctors were immediately sent for. They prescribed pills and powders, but nothing helped. They tried operating on one of the princes, but the ear they cut off grew back large as ever.

Mouk in his hideout heard what was happening at court and decided it was time to act. With the money he had received for the figs, he had provided himself with a new disguise. He was dressed like a doctor and wore a long beard of goat hair. He arrived at the palace carrying a sack of healing figs, said he was a doctor from another city, and offered his help. At first no one paid attention to him. But when he gave one of the princes a fig and his ears and nose became normal again, all the stricken clamoured to be cured, and Mouk gave them figs too.

The king, who out of shame no longer left his private quarters, summoned the foreign doctor and demanded to be cured at once. Mouk hesitated. When the king saw this, he came to him, took him by the hand and led him to a door which he unlocked. It was the door to his treasury and he beckoned Mouk to follow him in.

"Here are my treasures," said the impatient king. "You may choose whatever you wish if you cure me at once of this disgraceful affliction."

Mouk, who had spied his shoes and stick the moment he entered the room, walked around as if to inspect the king's treasures. As soon as he reached the magic shoes he slipped into them. He grabbed his stick, which lay nearby, pulled off his false beard, and revealed to the king the familiar face of Mouk, his banished messenger.

"Your Majesty," Mouk said, "you broke your word and rewarded faithful service with ingratitude. You deserve your punishment. Those ears and that nose will be a daily reminder of your Little Mouk."

Mouk quickly turned three times on his heel and wished himself far away. He was gone before the king could call for help.

In time Mouk returned to his town where he lived in comfort. Experience had made him a wise man. He earned the respect of his neighbours and was no longer scoffed at or ridiculed. Yet he continued to avoid people and to live alone for the rest of his years. He seldom left his house, but on fine evenings he could be seen walking up and down on his roof, his proud turbaned head showing just above the parapet.